William Winter

George William Curtis

A Eulogy

William Winter

George William Curtis
A Eulogy

ISBN/EAN: 9783743444010

Manufactured in Europe, USA, Canada, Australia, Japa

Cover: Foto ©Raphael Reischuk / pixelio.de

Manufactured and distributed by brebook publishing software
(www.brebook.com)

William Winter

George William Curtis

GEORGE WILLIAM CURTIS

𝔄 𝔈ulogy

*DELIVERED BEFORE THE PEOPLE OF STATEN
ISLAND, AT THE CASTLETON, ST. GEORGE,
FEBRUARY 24, 1893*

BY

WILLIAM WINTER

" Now is the stately column broke,
 The beacon-light is quench'd in smoke,
 The trumpet's silver sound is still,
 The warder silent on the hill."
                              Sir Walter Scott

PRINTED FOR THE

CURTIS COMMEMORATION COMMITTEE,
OF STATEN ISLAND,

BY

MACMILLAN AND CO.

NEW YORK AND LONDON

1893

GEORGE WILLIAM CURTIS.

This brilliant throng, this dazzling array of eager faces, this gentle, fervent welcome—they are not for me. They are for another. They proclaim your affectionate devotion to a gracious figure that has passed from this world; a voice that is silent; a face that here will shine on you no more. And, surely, if the souls of the departed are aware of anything upon this earth, if those ties of affection still subsist, without

which life—whether here or elsewhere—would be worthless, his
sacred spirit descends upon this
place, to-night, and sees into your
hearts and rejoices in your love,
and knows this hour and hallows
it.

In the days of my youth I was
often privileged to sit by the
fireside of the poet Longfellow.
He was exceedingly kind to me,
and with his encouragement and
under his guidance I entered
upon that service of literature
to which, humbly but earnestly, my life has been devoted.
Longfellow possessed a great
and peculiar fascination for
youth. He was a man who nat-

urally attracted to himself all unsophisticated spirits ; and—as I did not then know, but subsequently learned—he was a man who naturally attracted to himself all persons who were intrinsically noble. His gentleness was elemental. His tact was inerrant. His patience never failed. As I recall him I am conscious of a beautiful spirit; an altogether lovely life; a perfect image of continence, wisdom, dignity, sweetness, and grace. In Longfellow's home—the old Craigie mansion at Cambridge—on an autumn evening nearly forty years ago was assembled a brilliant company of gay ladies and

gallant gentlemen ; and as I entered the large drawing-room,
which now I believe is the library,
one figure in particular attracted
my gaze. It was a young man,
lithe, slender, faultlessly appar-
elled, very handsome, who rose
at my approach, turning upon
me a countenance that beamed
with kindness and a smile that
was a welcome from the heart.
His complexion was fair. His
hair was brown, long, and waving.
His features were regular and of
exquisite refinement. His eyes
were blue. His bearing was that
of manly freedom and unconven-
tional grace, and yet it was that
of absolute dignity. He had the

manner of the natural aristocrat—
a manner that is born, not made ;
a manner that is never found except in persons who are self-cen-
tred without being selfish ; who
are intrinsically noble, wholly simple and wholly true. I was in-
troduced to him by Longfellow :
and then and thus it was that
I first beheld George William
Curtis. From that hour until the
day he died I was honored with
his friendship—now become a hal-
lowed memory. That meeting
was more than once recalled between us ; and as I look back to
it, across the varied landscape of
intervening years, I see it as a
precious and altogether excep-

tional experience. It was a hand dispensing nothing but blessings which bestowed that incomparable boon—the illustrious and venerated hand of the foremost poet of America. It was the splendid magnificence of Longfellow that gave the benediction of Curtis.

It is not, however, only because he was a friend of mine that I have been asked to speak of him in this distinguished presence. It is because he was a friend of yours, whom you loved and honored living and whom you deplore in death. It is because he was a great person whose lot was cast in this community, and because this community is wishful to listen to even the humblest voice that can be raised in his honor. Not indeed that his name requires eulogy. The career of Curtis is rounded and complete. The splendid structure of his character stands before the world like a monument of gold. It is not for his sake that our tribute is laid upon the shrine of memory; it is for our own. When the grave has closed over one whom we love, our hearts instinctively strive to find a little comfort in the assurance that while it was yet possible to manifest our affection we did not fail to do so. 'We were never unkind' (so the heart whispers), 'we were never neglectful; we were always appreciative and sympathetic and true, and he was aware of our fidelity and found a pleasure in it.' By thoughts like those the sharpness of grief is dulled and the sense of loss is made less bitter. With that motive this assemblage has convened,—in order that here, amid the scenes that he knew and loved; here, within a few paces of the home that was so beautiful and is now so lonely; here, in the hall from which the echoes of his melodious voice have scarcely died away, his neighbors and friends, bringing their garlands of gentle remembrance and tender affection, may utter blessings on his name. It is the spirit of resignation for which we seek, and with it the satisfacfaction of our sense of duty. Not to express homage for a public benefactor would be to fail in self-respect. Not to reverence a noble and exemplary character is to · forego a benefit that is individual as well as social. Nowhere else can so much strength be derived as from the contemplation of men and women who pass through the vicissitudes of human experience,—the ordeal of life and death,—not without action and not without feeling, but calmly

and bravely, without fever and
without fear. There is nothing
greater in this world, nor can
there be anything greater in
the world to come, than a
perfectly pure and true and resolute soul. When the old Scotch
Lord Balmerino was going to
the block, on Tower Hill, — in
expiation of his alleged treason
to the House of Hanover,—he
spoke a few great words, that
ought to be forever remembered.
" The man who is not fit to die,"
he said, "is not fit to live."
That was the voice of a hero.
An image of heroism like that
is of inestimable value, and it
abides in the human soul as a

perpetual benediction. In Shakespeare's tragedy, when the foes of Brutus are seeking to capture him on the field of battle, his friend Lucilius, whom they have already taken, denotes, in two consummate lines, the same inspiring ideal of superb stability:

" When you do find him, or alive
   or dead,
He will be found like Brutus, like
   himself."

That might always have been said of Curtis. That was the man whom we admired and loved. That was the character we do ourselves the justice to celebrate and reverence now. In every duty faithful; in every trial adequate; in every attribute of nobility perfect—

"He taught us how to live, and—oh, too high
The price for knowledge!—taught us how to die."

And that announces to you the substance and the drift of my discourse. It is not the achievement of Curtis that now lingers most lovingly in the memory—it is the character. The authoritative and final word upon his works will be spoken by posterity. For us it is enough that we remind each

other of what we already know
of the man. . . . "When a neigh-
bor dies" (so Curtis himself
wrote, in his wise and sympathetic sketch of the beloved and
lamented Theodore Winthrop),
"his form and quality appear
clearly, as if he had been dead
a thousand years. Then we see
what we only felt before. Heroes in history seem to us poetic because they are there. But
if we should tell the simple truth
of some of our neighbors it
would sound like poetry." . . .
The simple truth about Curtis
has that sound now, and more
and more it will have that sound
as time proceeds. It is the

story of a man of genius whose pure life and splendid powers were devoted to the ministry of beauty and to the self-sacrificing service of mankind. The superficial facts of that story, indeed, are familiar and usual. It was the inspiration of them that made them poetic—that profound, intuitive sense of the obligation of noble living which controlled and fashioned and directed his every thought and deed. The incidents customary in the life of a man of letters are scarcely more important than were the migrations of the Vicar of Wakefield from the brown bed to the blue and from the blue bed back again to the brown. He moves from place to place; he has ill fortune and good fortune; he gains and loses; he rejoices and suffers; he writes books: and he is never justly appreciated until he is dead. Curtis was a man of letters, born sixty-nine years ago this day, in our American Venice, the New England city of Providence; born nearly two months before the death of Byron (so near, in literature, we always are to the great names of the past), —and a boy of eight in that dark year which ended the illustrious lives of Goethe and Sir Walter Scott. It has been usual

to ascribe the direction of his
career to the influence of his
juvenile experience at Brook
Farm, in Roxbury, where he
resided from 1840 to 1844; but
it should be remembered that
the Brook Farm ideal was in his
mind before he went there—the
ideal of a social existence regu-
lated by absolute justice and
adorned by absolute beauty. In
that idyllic retreat—that earthly
Eden, conceived and founded by
the learned and gentle George
Ripley as a home for all the
beatitudes and all the arts —
and later, at Concord, his young
mind, no doubt, was stimulated
by some of the most invigo-

rating forces that ever were liberated upon human thought: Theodore Parker, who was incarnate truth; the mystical spirit of Channing; the resolute, intrepid, humanitarian Dana; the sombre, imaginative Hawthorne; the audacious intellect and indomitable will of Margaret Fuller; and, greatest of all, the heaveneyed thought of Emerson. But the preordination of that mind to the service of justice and beauty and humanity was germinal in itself. Curtis began wisely, because he followed the star of his own destiny. He was wise, in boyhood, when he went to Brook Farm. He was wiser still in early manhood,—having formally adopted the vocation of literature,—when he sought the haunted lands of the Orient, and found inspiration and theme in subjects that were novel because their scene was both august and remote.   On that expedition, consuming four precious years, he penetrated into the country of the Nile and he roamed in Arabia and Syria.   He stood before the Sphinx and he knelt at the Holy Sepulchre in Jerusalem. It is a privilege to be able to add—since he was an American —that he did not endeavor to be comic.   When, in later days,

my friend Artemus Ward went
to the Tower of London he
looked upon the Traitor's Gate,
and he remarked that apparent-
ly as many as twenty traitors
might go in abreast. It was
funny—but to a reverent mind
the note is a discordant note.
Curtis was a humorist, but he
was not the humorist who grins
amid the sculptures of Westmin-
ster Abbey. He was a humorist
as Addison was, whom he much
resembled. He looked upon life
with tranquil, pensive, kindly
eyes. He exulted in all of
goodness that it contains; he
touched its foibles with bland,
whimsical drollery; he would

have made all persons happy by making them all noble, serene, gentle, and patient. Such a mind could degrade nothing. Least of all could it degrade dignity with sport, or antiquity with ridicule. He looked at the statue of Memnon and he saw that "serene repose is the attitude and character of godlike grandeur." "Those forms," he said, "impress man with himself. In them we no longer succumb to the landscape, but sit, individual and imperial, under the sky, by the mountains and the river. Man is magnified in Memnon." He stood among the ruined temples of Erment and

he saw Cleopatra, glorious in
beauty upon the throne of Rame-
ses, and he uttered neither a
scrap of morality nor a figment
of jest. " Nothing Egyptian,"
he said, "is so cognate to our
warm human sympathy as the
rich romance of Cleopatra and
her Roman lovers." . . . " The
great persons and events," he
added, "that notch time in passing do so because Nature gave
them such an excessive and ex-
aggerated impulse that wherever
they touch they leave their
mark ; and that intense humanity secures human sympathy beyond the most beautiful balance,
which, indeed, the angels love

and we are beginning to appreci-
ate." That was the spirit in which
he rambled and saw and wrote.
"The highest value of travel," he
urged, "is not the accumulation
of facts, but the perception of
their significance." In those true
words he made his comment, not
simply upon the immediate and
local scene, but upon the whole
wide stage of human activity
and experience. He was wise,
when he began to labor for the
present, thus to fortify himself
with the meaning of the past.
Those early books of his, the
"Nile Notes" and the "Howadji
in Syria,"—which have been before the world for more than

forty years,—will always be a refreshment and a delight. They glow with the authentic vitality of nature,—her warmth, and color, and copious profusion, and exultant joy,—and they are buoyant with the ardor of an auspicious and yet unsaddened soul. But they are exceptionally precious now, for their guidance to the springs of his character. In the "Syria" there is a passage that, perhaps, furnishes the key to his whole career. He is speaking of successful persons, and he says this: . . . "Success is a delusion. It is an attainment— but who attains? It is the horizon, always bounding our path and therefore never gained. The Pope, triple-crowned, and borne, with flabella, through St. Peter's, is not successful,—for he might be canonized into a saint. Pygmalion, before his perfect statue, is not successful,—for it might live. Raphael, finishing the Sistine Madonna, is not successful,—for her beauty has revealed to him a finer and an unattainable beauty." ... In those words you perceive, at the outset, the spirit of comprehensive, sweet, and tolerant reason that was ever the conspicuous attribute of his mind. Those words denote, indeed, the inherent forces that governed him to the last—perception and practical remembrance of what has already been accomplished, and the realization that human life is not final achievement but endless endeavor.

In early days Curtis wrote verse, as well as prose. As late as 1863 he delivered before the Sons of Rhode Island a poem of 418 lines, entitled " A Rhyme of Rhode Island and the Times." In that occurs his impassioned pæan for the Flag of the Republic :

" At last, at last, each glowing star
In that pure field of heavenly blue,
On every people shining far,
Burns, to its utmost promise
true. . . .

"And when the hour seems dark
    with doom
  Our sacred banner, lifted higher,
Shall flash away the gathering
    gloom
  With inextinguishable fire.

"Pure as its white the future see!
  Bright as its red is now the sky!
Fixed as its stars the faith shall
    be
  That nerves our hands to do or
    die!"

Those are but three of the
eight stanzas. They show his
patriotic ardor, and they also
show the felicity of his diction
in verse. That felicity is still
further manifested in another

characteristic passage, denoting
that in the eighteenth-century
manner he also could have been
expert, if he had cared to pur-
sue it :

" Admonished, by life's fluctuating
    scene,
Of all he is and all he might have
    been,
Man, toiling upward on the dizzy
    track,
Still looks regretful or remorseful
    back ;
Paces old paths, remembering vows
    that rolled
In burning words from hearts for-
    ever cold ;
Bows his sad head where once he
    bowed the knee

And kissed the lips that no more
   kissed shall be.
So the sad traveller climbing from
   the plain
Turns from the hill and sees his
   home again,
And sighs to know that,—this sweet
   prospect o'er,—
The boundless world is but a foreign
   shore."

A certain frenzy is inseparable
from the temperament of the
poet. He must not yield his
mind absolutely to its control,
but he must be capable of it
and he must guide and direct
its course. He must not, with
Savage and with Burns, abdi-
cate the supremacy of the soul.

He must, with Shakespeare and
with Goethe (to borrow the fine
figure of Addison), "ride on the
whirlwind and direct the storm."
The conduct of his life must not
be a delirium; but the capacity
of delirium must, inevitably, be
a part of his nature. Conven-
tionality is bounded by four
walls. Unless the heart of the
poet be passionate he cannot
move the hearts of others: and
the poet who does not touch the
heart is a poet of no impor-
tance. Curtis was a man of deep
poetic sensibility. In that idyllic
composition, "Prue and I," the
poetic atmosphere is invariably
sustained and it is invariably

beautiful. The use of poetic quotation, wherever it occurs, throughout his writings, is remarkably felicitous—as in his book that we know as "Lotus-Eating," written in 1851—and it manifests the keenest appreciation of the poetic element. His analysis of the genius of Bryant, in his noble oration before the Century Club in 1878, is not less subtle than potential, and it leaves nothing to be said. His perception of the ideal—as when he wrote upon Hamlet, with the spiritual mind and prince-like figure of Edwin Booth in that character—was equally profound and comprehensive, and as fine and delicate as it was unerringly true. There can be little doubt that he was conscious, originally, of a strong impulse toward poetry, but that this was restricted. and presently was diverted into other channels, partly by the stress of his philosophical temperament, and partly by the untoward force of iron circumstance. His nature was not without fervor; but it was the fervor of moral and spiritual enthusiasm, not of passion. His faculties and feelings were exquisitely poised, and I do not think there ever was a time in all his life when that perfect sanity was disturbed by any inordinate waywardness or any blast of storm. The benign and potent but utterly dispassionate influence of Emerson touched his responsive spirit, at the beginning of his career, and beneath that mystic and wonderful spell of Oriental contemplation and bland and sweet composure his destiny was fulfilled. Like gravitates to like. Each individual sways by that power, whatsoever it be, to which in nature he is the most closely attuned. The poetic voice of Emerson was the voice, not of the human heart, but of the pantheistic spirit:

" As sunbeams stream through liberal space,

And nothing jostle nor displace,
So waved the pine-tree through my
    thought,
And fanned the dreams it never
    brought."

In Curtis the poetic voice was
less remote and more human ; but
it was of the same elusive quality. It was not often heard. It
sounded very sweetly in his tender
lyric of other days :

" Sing the song that once you sung,
    When we were together young,
    When there were but you and I
    Underneath the summer sky.

" Sing the song, and o'er and o'er—
    But I know that nevermore
    Will it be the song you sung
    When we were together young."

There can be no higher mission than that of the poet, but there are many vocations that exact more direct practical effort and involve more immediate practical results. One of those vocations, meanwhile, had largely absorbed the mind of Curtis.

To people of the present day it would be difficult to impart an adequate idea of the state of political feeling that existed in New England forty years ago. The passage of the Fugitive Slave Act, which was regarded as the culmination of a long series of encroachments, had inspired a tremendous resentment, and the community there was seething with bitterness and conflict. The novel of " Uncle Tom's Cabin " had blazoned the national crime of slavery, and had aroused and inflamed thousands of hearts against it, as a sin and a disgrace. Theodore Parker—that moral and intel-,lectual giant—was preaching in the Boston Music Hall. The passionate soul of Thomas Starr King poured forth its melodious fervor in the old church in Hollis Street. Sumner, and Phillips, and Wilson, and Giddings, and Hale, and Burlingame, in Faneuil Hall and everywhere else, were pleading the cause of the slave and the purification of the flag. The return of Anthony Burns from Boston, in

June, 1854,—when the court-house
was surrounded with chains and
soldiers, and when State Street
was commanded with cannon,—
although perfectly legal, was felt
by every freeman as an act of
monstrous tyranny, and as the
consummation of national shame.
The murderous assault on Sumner,
committed in the United States
Senate chamber by Brooks of
South Carolina, had aroused all
that was best of manly pride
and moral purpose in the North,
and from the moment when that
blow was struck every man who
was not blinded by folly knew that
the end of human slavery in the
Republic must inevitably come.

There never had been seen in our political history so wild a tide of enthusiasm as that which swept through the New England States, bearing onward the standard of Frémont, in 1856. Statesmen, indeed, there were—foreseeing and dreading civil war—who steadily counselled moderation and compromise. Edward Everett was one of those pacificators, and Rufus Choate was another. Choate, in Faneuil Hall, delivered one of the most enchanting orations of his life, in solemn and passionate warning against those impetuous zealots of freedom who—as he beheld them—were striving to rend asunder the colossal crag of national unity, al-

ready smitten by the lightning and
riven from summit to base. And
it must be admitted—and it needs
no apology—that the conviction
of generous patriotism in those wild
days of wrath and tempest was the
conviction that a Union under
which every citizen of every free
State was, by the law, made a hun-
ter of negro slaves for a Southern
driver, was not only worthless but
infamous. Conservatives, cynics,
mercenary, scheming politicians,
and timid friends of peace might
hesitate, and palter with the occa-
sion, and seek to evade the issue and
postpone the struggle ; but the
general drift of New England sentiment was all the other way. Old

political lines disappeared. The
everlasting bickerings of Protes-
tant and Catholic were for a moment hushed. The Know-Nothings
vanished. The thin ghosts of the
old silver-gray Whig party, led by
Bell and Everett, moaned feebly
at parting and faded into air.
Elsewhere in the nation the lines
of party conflict were sharply
drawn ; but in New England
one determination animated every
bosom — the determination that
human slavery should perish. The
spirit that walked abroad was the
spirit of Concord Bridge and Bun-
ker Hill. The silent voices of
Samuel Adams and James Otis
were silent no more. "My ances-

tor fell at Lexington," said old Joel Parker—then over threescore years of age—"and I am ready to shed more of the same blood in the same cause." It was a tremendous epoch in New England history, and we who were youths in it felt our hearts aflame with holy ardor in a righteous cause. I was myself a follower of the Pathfinder and a speaker for him, in that stormy time,—assailing Choate and Caleb Cushing and other giants of the adverse faction, with the freedom and confidence that are possible only to unlimited moral enthusiasm. What a different world it was from the world of to-day ! How sure we were that all we desired to do was wise and right! How plainly we saw our duty, and how eager we were for the onset and the strife! If we could only have foreseen the beatific condition of the present, I wonder if that zeal would have cooled. Some of us have grown a little weary of rolling the Sisyphus stone of benevolence for the aggrandizement of a selfish multitude, careless of everything except its sensual enjoyment. But it was a glorious enthusiasm while it lasted; and, as poor Byron truly said,

"There's not a joy the world can give
    like that it takes away,
When the glow of early thought declines in feeling's dull decay."

Into that conflict, of Right against Wrong, Curtis threw himself with all his soul. His reputation as a speaker had already been established. He had made his first public address in 1851 before the New York National Academy of Design—discussing " Contemporary Artists of Europe,"—and in 1853 he had formally adopted the Platform as a vocation; and it continued to be a part of his vocation for the next twenty years. He was everywhere popular in the lyceum, and he now brought into the more turbulent field of politics the dignity of the scholar, the refinement and grace of the gentleman, and all the varied equipments of the zealous and accomplished advocate, the caustic satirist, and the impassioned champion of the rights of man. I first heard him speak on politics—making an appeal for Frémont—at a popular convention in the town of Fitchburg. It was on a summer day, under canvas, but almost in the open air. The assemblage was vast. Curtis followed Horace Greeley — with whose peculiar drawl and rustic aspect his princelike demeanor and lucid and sonorous rhetoric were in wonderful contrast. Neither of those men was wordly-wise ; neither was versed in political duplicity. Greeley, no doubt, had then the

advantage in political wisdom ;
but Curtis was the orator—and,
while Curtis spoke, the hearts of
that multitude were first lured and
entranced by the golden tones of
his delicious voice, and then were
shaken, as with a whirlwind, by
the righteous fervor of his magnificent enthusiasm. It was the
diamond morning blaze of that
perfect eloquence which some of
you have known in its noonday
splendor, and all of you have
known in its sunset ray. He
continued to speak for that cause
—everywhere with great effect;
and down to the war-time, and
during the war-time, the principles which are at the basis of

the American Republic had no champion more eloquent or more sincere. He abandoned the platform as a regular employment in 1873; but—as we all gratefully remember—he never altogether ceased the exercise of that matchless gift of oratory for which he was remarkable and by which he was enabled to accomplish so much good and diffuse so much happiness.

In this domain he came to his zenith. The art in which Curtis excelled all his contemporaries of the last thirty years was the art of oratory. Many other authors wrote better in verse, and some others wrote as well in prose.

Hawthorne, Motley, Lowell, Whipple, Giles, Mitchell, Warner, and Stedman were masters of style. But in the felicity of speech Curtis was supreme above all other men of his generation. My reference is to the period from 1860 to 1890. Oratory as it existed in America in the previous epoch has no living representative. Curtis was the last orator of the great school of Everett, Sumner, and Wendell Phillips. His model —in so far as he had a model —was Sumner, and the style of Sumner was based on Burke. But Curtis had heard more magical voices than those—for he had heard Daniel Webster and Rufus

Choate ; and although he was
averse to their politics, he could
profit by their example. Webster
and Choate—each in a different
way—were perfection. The eloquence of Webster had the af-
fluent potentiality of the rising
sun ; of the lonely mountain ; of
the long, regular, successive
surges of the resounding sea. His
periods were as lucid as the light.
His logic was irresistible. His
facts came on in a solid phalanx of
overwhelming power. His tones
were crystal-clear. His magnificent person towered in dignity
and seemed colossal in its imperial
grandeur. His voice grew in
volume, as he became more and

more aroused, and his language glowing with the fire of conviction, rose and swelled and broke, like the great ninth wave that shakes the solid crag. His speech, however, was addressed always to the reason, never to the imagination. The eloquence of Rufus Choate, on the other hand, was the passionate enchantment of the actor and the poet—an eloquence in which you felt the rush of the tempest, and heard the crash of breakers and the howling of frantic gales and the sobbing wail of homeless winds in bleak and haunted regions of perpetual night. He began calmly, often in a tone that was hardly more than a whisper; but as he proceeded the whole man was gradually absorbed and transfigured, as into a fountain of fire, which then poured forth, in one tumultuous and overwhelming torrent of melody, the iridescent splendors of description, and appeal, and humor, and pathos, and invective, and sarcasm, and poetry, and beauty—till the listener lost all consciousness of self and was borne away as on a golden river flowing to a land of dreams. The vocabulary of that orator seemed literally to have no limit. His voice sounded every note, from a low, piercing whisper to a shrill, sonorous scream.   His remarkable appearance, further-more, enhanced the magic of his speech.   The tall, gaunt, vital figure, the symmetrical head, the clustered hair,—once black, now faintly touched with gray,—the emaciated, haggard countenance, the pallid olive complexion, the proud Arabian features, the mournful flaming brown eyes, the imperial demeanor and wild and lawless grace—all those at-tributes of a strange, poetic per-sonality commingled with the boundless resources of his elo-quence to rivet the spell of alto-gether exceptional character and genius.   In singular contrast with Choate was still another great orator whom Curtis heard, — and about whom he has written, — that consummate scholar and rhetorician Edward Everett. There is no statelier figure in American history. If Everett had been as puissant in character as he was ample in scholarship, and as rich in emotion as he was fine in intellect, he would have been the peerless wonder of the age. He was a person of singular beauty. His form was a little above the middle height and perfectly proportioned. His head was beautifully formed and exquisitely poised. His closely clustering hair was as

white as silver. His features
were regular; his eyes were dark;
his countenance was pale, refined,
and cold. His aspect was formal
and severe. He dressed habitu-
ally in black, — often wearing
around his neck a thin gold
chain, outside of his coat. His
eloquence was the perfection of
art. I heard him often, and in
every one of his orations,—except
the magnificent one that he gave
in Faneuil Hall on the death of
Rufus Choate, which was supreme and without blemish,—his
art was distinctly obvious. He
began in a level tone and with a
formal manner. He spoke without a manuscript, and whether his

speech was long or short he never missed a word nor made an error. As he proceeded his countenance kindled and his figure began to move. With action he was profuse, and every one of his gestures had the beauty of a mathematical curve and the certainty of a mathematical demonstration. His movement suited his word, his pauses were exactly timed; his finely modulated voice rose and fell with rhythmic beat; and his polished periods flowed from his lips with limpid fluency and delicious cadence. A distinguishing attribute of his art was its elaborate complexity. In his noble oration on Washington, when he came to contrast the honesty of that patriot with the mercenary greed of Marlborough, it was not with words alone that he pointed his moral, but with a graceful, energetic blow upon his pocket that mingled the jingle of coin with the accents of scorn. One speech of his I remember (as far back as 1852) contained a description of the visible planets and constellations in the midnight sky; and his verbal pageantry was so magnificent that almost, I thought, it might take its place among them.

Such was the school of oratory in which Curtis studied and in which his style was formed. It no longer exists. The oratory of the present day is characterized by colloquialism, familiarity, and comic anecdote. Curtis maintained the dignity of the old order. You all remember the charm of his manner—how subtle it was, yet seemingly how simple ; how completely it convinced and satisfied you ; how it clarified your intelligence ; how it ennobled your mood. One secret of it, no doubt, was its perfect sincerity. Noble himself, and speaking only for right, and truth, and beauty, he addressed nobility in others. That consideration would explain the moral and the genial authority of his eloquence. The total effect of it, however, was attributable to his exquisite and inexplicable art. He could make an extemporaneous speech, but as a rule his speeches were carefully prepared. They had not always been written, but they had always been composed and considered. He possessed absolute self-control; a keen sense of symmetry and proportion; the faculty of logical thought and lucid statement; unbounded resources of felicitous illustration; passionate earnestness, surpassing sweetness of speech, and perfect grace of action. Like Everett,—whom he more closely resembled than he

did any other of the great masters of oratory,—he could trust
his memory and he could trust
his composure. He began with
the natural deference of un-
studied courtesy — serene, pro-
pitiatory, irresistibly winning.
He captured the eye and the ear
upon the instant, and before he
had been speaking for many
minutes he captured the heart.
There was not much action in
his delivery ; there never was any
artifice.   His gentle tones grew
earnest.   His fine face became
illumined.   His golden periods
flowed with more and more of
impetuous force, and the climax
of their perfect music was always

exactly identical with the climax of their thought. There always was a certain culmination of fervent power at which he aimed, and after that a gradual subsidence to the previous level of gracious serenity. He created and sustained the absolute illusion of spontaneity. You never felt that you had been beguiled by art: you only felt that you had been entranced by nature. I never could explain it to myself. I cannot explain it to you. I can only say of him, as he himself said of Wendell Phillips: "The secret of the rose's sweetness, of the bird's ecstasy, of the sunset's glory—that is the secret of genius and of eloquence."

While, however, the secret of his eloquence was elusive, the purpose and effect of it were perfectly clear. It dignified the subject and it ennobled the hearer. He once told me of a conversation, about poetry and oratory, between himself and the late distinguished senator, Roscoe Conkling. That statesman, having declared that, in his judgment, the perfection of poetry was " Casabianca," by Mrs. Hemans (" The boy stood on the burning deck "), and the perfection of oratory a passage in a Fourth-of-July oration by Charles

Sprague, desired Curtis to name
a supreme specimen of eloquence.
" I mentioned," said Curtis, "a
passage in Emerson's Dartmouth
College oration,—in which, however, Mr. Conkling could perceive
no peculiar force." That passage
Curtis proceeded to repeat to me.
I wish that I could say it as it
was said by him ; but that is im-
possible. Yet the citation of it is
appropriate, not only as showing
his ideal but as explaining his
self-devotion, not to art alone but
to conscience.

"You will hear every day"
(so runs that pearl of noble
thought and feeling) "the max-
ims of a low prudence. You

will hear that the first duty is to get land and money, place and name. 'What is this Truth you seek? what is this Beauty?' men will ask, with derision. If, nevertheless, God have called any of you to explore truth and beauty, be bold, be firm, be true! When you shall say, 'As others do, so will I; I renounce, I am sorry for it, my early visions; I must eat the good of the land and let learning and romantic expectation go until a more convenient season;'—then dies the man in you; then once more perish the buds of art and poetry and science, as they have died already in a thousand, thousand hearts. The hour of that choice is the crisis of your history: and see that you hold yourself fast by the intellect." . . . It was natural that Curtis should adopt that doctrine. He would have evolved it if he had not found it. That divine law was in his nature, and from that divine law he never swerved.

How should a man of genius use his gift? Setting aside the restrictive pressure of circumstance, two ways are open to him. He may cultivate himself standing aloof from the world, as Goethe did and as Tennyson did,—aiming to make his powers of expression perfect, and to make his expression itself universal, potential, irresistible, such as will sift into the lives of the human race as sunshine sifts into the trees of the forest; or he may take an executive course and yoke himself to the plough and the harrow, aiming to exert an immediate influence upon his environment. The former way is not at once comprehended by the world : the latter is more obvious.

In his poem of Retaliation, Goldsmith has designated Edmund Burke as a man who,

" Born for the universe, narrowed his
    mind,

And to party gave up what was
meant for mankind."

It has always seemed to me
that Curtis made one sacrifice
when he went into business, and
another when he went into politics. He manifested, indeed, ster-
ling character and splendid abil-
ity in both ; yet he did not, in
a practical sense, succeed in
either. The end of his experi-
ment in business was a heavy
burden of debt, which he was
compelled to bear through a
long period of anxious and
strenuous toil. His experience
was not the terrible experience
of Sir Walter Scott—that heroic
gentleman, that supreme and in-

comparable magician of romance!
—but it was an experience of
the same kind. He released himself from his burden, justly and
honorably, at last ; but the strain
upon his mind was an injury to
him, and I believe that the literature of his country is poorer
because of the sacrifice that he
was obliged to make. That
"Life of Mehemet Ali," the great
Pasha of Egypt, which he de-
signed to write, was never written. On a day in 1860 I met
him in Broadway, and he said
to me, very earnestly, "Take advantage of the moment: don't
delay too long that fine poem,
that great novel, that you in-

tend to write." It was the wise philosophy that takes heed of the enormous values of youth and freedom. It pleases some philosophers, indeed, to believe that a man of letters will accomplish his best expression when goaded by what Shakespeare calls "the thorny point of sharp necessity." That practice of glorifying hardship is sometimes soothing to human vanity. Men have thought themselves heroes because they rise early. It may possibly be true of the poets that they learn in suffering what they teach in song; but the suffering must not be sordid. Literature was never yet enriched through the pressure of want. The author may write more, because of his need, but he will not write better. The best literatures of the world, the literatures of Greece and England, were created in the gentlest and most propitious climates of the world. The best individual works in those literatures—with little exception—were produced by writers whose physical circumstances were those of comfort and peace. Chaucer, Shakespeare, Milton, Herrick, Addison, Pope, Byron, Wordsworth, Shelley, Scott, Moore, Lamb, Thackeray, Tennyson—neither of them lacked

the means of reputable subsist-
ence. Burns, fine as he was,
would have been finer still, in a
softer and sweeter environment
of worldly circumstance. Curtis
was a man of extraordinary patience, concentration, and poise.
He accepted the conditions in
which he found himself, and he
made the best of them. His in-
cessant industry and his composure, to the last, were prodigious.
He never, indeed, was acquainted
with want. The shackle that business imposed on him was the
shackle of drudgery. He was
compelled to write profusely and
without pause. His pen was never
at rest. Once—in 1873—he broke

down completely, and for several months he could not work at all. During more than forty years, however, he worked all the time. Curtis, at his best, had the grace of Addison, the kindness of Steele, the simplicity of Goldsmith, and the nervous force of the incomparable Sterne. Writing under such conditions, however, no man can always be at his best. The wonder is that his average was so fine. He attained to a high and orderly level of wise and kindly thought, of gentle fancy, and of winning ease, and he steadily maintained it. He had an exceptional faculty for choosing diversified themes, and his treatment of them was always felicitous. He wrought in many moods, but always genially and without flurry, and he gave the continuous impression of spontaneity and pleasure. A fetter, however, is not the less a fetter because it is lightly borne, and whatever is easy to read was hard to write. It may be, of course, that the troublesome business experience in the life of Curtis was only an insignificant incident. It may be that he fulfilled himself as an author—leaving nothing undone that he had the power to do. But that is not my reading of the artistic mind, and it is not my reading of him. For me the mist was drawn too early across those luminous and tender pictures of the Orient, those haunting shapes and old historic splendors of the Nile. For me the rich, tranquil note of tender music that breathes in " Prue and I" was too soon hushed and changed. Genius is the petrel, and like the petrel it loves the freedom of the winds and waves.

" My thoughts like swallows skim the
        main,
  And bear my spirit back again,
  Over the earth and through the air—
  A wild bird and a wanderer."

All thinkers repudiate the narrow philosophy that would regulate one man's life by the standard of another. " Be yourself!" is the precept of the highest wisdom. Shakespeare has written his Plays. Milton has written his Epic. Those things cannot be done again and should not be expected. The new genius must mount upon its own wings, and hold its own flight, and seek the eyrie that best it loves. I recognize, and feel, and honor the nobility of Curtis as a citizen; but I cannot cast aside the regret that he did not dedicate himself exclusively to Literature. Everything is relative. To such a nature as that of Curtis the pursuits of business and politics are foreign

and inappropriate. He was un-
doubtedly equal to all their
responsibilities and duties; but
he was equal to much more—to
things different and higher—and
the practical service essential to
business and politics did not
need him. The State, indeed,
needs the virtue that he possessed
—but needs it in the form, not of
the poet but the gladiator, who,
when he goes rejoicing to battle,
has no harp to leave in silence
and no garlands to cast unheeded
in the dust. I would send Saint
Peter, with his sword, to the pri-
mary meeting; I would not send
the apostle John. The organist
should not be required to blow

the bellows. Curtis was, by nature, a man of letters. His faculty in that direction was prodigious. So good a judge as
Thackeray, looking at him as a
young man, declared him to be
the most auspicious of all our
authors. It is a great vocation,
and because its force, like that of
nature, is deep, slow, silent, and
elemental, it is the most tremendous force concerned in human
affairs. Shall I try to say what it
is? The mission of the man of
letters is to touch the heart; to
kindle the imagination; to en-
noble the mind. He is the inter-
preter between the spirit of
beauty that is in nature and the

general intelligence and sensibility of mankind. He sets to music the pageantry and the pathos of human life, and he keeps alive in the soul the holy enthusiasm of devotion to the ideal. He honors and perpetuates heroic conduct, and he teaches, by many devices of art—by story, and poem, and parable, and essay, and drama— purity of life, integrity to man, and faith in God. He is continu- ally reminding you of the good- ness and loveliness to which you may attain ; continually causing you to see what opportunities of nobility your life affords ; continu- ally delighting you with high thoughts and beautiful pictures.

He does not preach to you. He
does not attempt to regulate your
specific actions. He does not
assail you with the hysterical
scream of the reformer. He does
not carp, and vex, and meddle.
He whispers to you, in your silent
hours, of love and heroism and
holiness and immortality, and you
are refreshed and strong, and
come forth into the world smiling
at fortune and bearing blessings
in your hands. On these bleak
February nights, with the breakers
clashing on our icy coasts and the
trumpets of the wind resounding
in our chimneys, how sweet it has
been, sitting by the evening lamp,
to turn the pages of "The Tem-

pest," or "The Antiquary," or
"Old Mortality," or "Henry Es-
mond," or "The Idylls of the
King," while the treasured faces
of Shakespeare and Scott and
Thackeray and Tennyson looked
down from the library walls!
How sweet to read those tender, romantic, imaginative pages
of "Prue and I," in which the
pansies and the rosemary bloom
forever, and to think of him who
wrote them!

"His presence haunts this room to-
    night,—
A form of mingled mist and light
    From that far coast!
Welcome beneath this roof of mine!
Welcome! this vacant chair is thine,
    Dear guest and ghost."

But whether the choice that Curtis made was a sacrifice or not, we know he made it and we know why he made it. Prefigured in his character and his writings, at the outset, and illustrated in all his conduct, was the supreme law of his being—practical consideration for others. The trouble of the world was his trouble. The disciple of Andrew Marvel could not rest at ease in the summer - land of Keats. His heart was there; but his duty, as he saw it, steadily called him away.

"Some life of men unblest
He knew, which made him droop, and fill'd his head.

He went; his piping took a troubled
    sound,
Of storms that rage outside our
    happy ground;
He could not wait their passing; he
    is dead."

He would have rejoiced in
writing more books like "Prue
and I;" but the virtuous glory
of the commonwealth and the
honor and happiness of the people were forever present to him,
as the first and the most solemn
responsibility. When his proto-
type, Sir Philip Sidney, on that
fatal September morning, three
hundred and seven years ago,
set forth for the field of battle
at Zutphen, he met a fellow-

soldier riding in light armor, and thereupon he cast away a portion of his own mail—and in so doing, as the event proved, he cast away his life—in order that he might be no better protected than his friend. In like manner Curtis would have no advantage for himself, nor even the semblance of advantage, that was not shared by others. He could not—with his superlative moral fervor—dedicate himself exclusively to letters, while there was so much wrong in the world that clamored for him to do his part in setting it right. He believed that his direct, practical labor was essential and

would avail, and he was eager
to bestow it. Men of strong
imagination begin life with il-
limitable ideals, with vast illu-
sions, with ardent and generous
faith. They are invariably disappointed, and they are usually
embittered. Curtis was controlled less by his imagination
than by his moral sense. He
had ideals, but they were based
on reason. However much he
may have loved to muse and
dream, he saw the world as a
fact and not as a fancy. He
was often saddened by the spec-
tacle of human littleness, but,
broadly and generally, he was
not disappointed in mankind,

and he never became embittered.
The belief in human nature with
which he began remained his
belief when he ended. Nothing
could shake his conviction that
man is inherently and intrinsically good. He believed in the
people. He believed in earthly
salvation for the poor, the weak,
and the oppressed. He believed
in chivalry toward woman. He
believed in refinement, gentleness, and grace. He believed
that the world is growing better
and not worse. He believed in
the inevitable, final triumph of
truth and right over falsehood
and wrong. He believed in freedom, charity, justice, hope, and

love. The last line that fell from the dying pen of Longfellow might have been the last word that fell from the dying lips of Curtis: " 'Tis daylight everywhere!"

Upon the spirit in which he served the state no words can make so clear a comment as his own. "There is no nobler ambition," he said, "than to fill a great office greatly." His estimate of Bryant culminates in the thought that "no man, no American, living or dead, has more truly and amply illustrated the scope and fidelity of republican citizenship." . . . "The great argument for popular government," he declared, in his fine eulogy on Wendell Phillips, " is not the essential righteousness of a majority, but the celestial law which subordinates the brute force of numbers to intellectual and moral ascendency." And his stately tribute to the character of Washington reached a climax in his impassioned homage to its lofty serenity, its moral grandeur, and its majestic repose. The quality of every man may be divined from the objects of his genuine devotion. There could be no doubt of the patriotism of Curtis : and I will make bold to say that, in the conditions which

now confront the American Republic,—conditions more perilous
than ever yet existed in its
experience (vicious immigration,
the dangerous Indian, the still
more dangerous negro, racial
antagonism, discontented labor,
socialism, communism, anarchy,
a licentious press, a tottering
church, ambitious Roman Cathol-
icism, the Irish vote, boss rule,
ring rule, corruption in office,
levity, profanity, and a generally
low state of public morals),—it
was no slight thing that such
a man as Curtis should have
testified, to the last, his confidence in the future of the American people, and to the last

should have devoted his splendid powers more largely to their practical service than to anything else. Fortunate is the man who can close the awfully true book of "Ecclesiastes" and forget its terrible lessons! Fortunate is the people that has the example, the sympathy, the support, and the guidance of such a man! If the altogether high and noble principles that Curtis advocated could prevail, then indeed the Republic that Washington conceived would be a glorious reality. When a wise and final check is placed upon the influence of mere numbers —then, and not till then, will

the ideal of Washington be fulfilled ; then, and not till then,
will the Republic be safe. There
is no belief more delusive and per-
nicious than the belief that virtue
and wisdom are resident in the
will of the multitude.

If, therefore, Curtis made a
sacrifice in turning from the Muse
to labor for the commonwealth,
at least it was not made in vain.
Nor must it be forgotten that—
despite his preoccupation as a
publicist and as the incumbent
of many unpaid and most exact-
ing offices—his contributions to
literature, especially in the domain
of the Essay, were extraordinary
and brilliant. When, in 1846, he

began his literary career, a young
man of twenty-two, American literature had begun to assume the
proportions of a substantial and
impressive fabric.   Paulding, Irving, Dana, Bryant, Cooper, and
Percival were in the zenith. Longfellow and Whittier were ascending.
Hawthorne was slowly becoming
an auspicious figure.   Halleck and
George Fenno Hoffman were reign-
ing poets. Poe had nearly finished,
in penniless obscurity, his desolate
strife.   Holmes, aged 37, was but
little beyond the threshold : and
the fine genius of Stoddard was
yet unknown. Griswold still held
the sceptre, which Willis was presently to inherit. Allston and Paul-

ding were 67 years old ; Irving was
63 ; R. H. Dana was 59 ; Sprague
54; Bryant 51; Drake, Halleck, and
Percival 50. Emerson was only 42.
Into that company Curtis entered,
as a boy among graybeards. Authors were more numerous than
they had been thirty years earlier,
but they were less numerous than
they are now, and, perhaps, less
distinctive. It was easier to ac-
quire literary reputation then than
it is at present ; but genuine literary reputation was never easily
obtained. Curtis made a new
mark. In his oriental travels the
observation was large ; the fancy
delicate ; the feeling deep ; the
touch light. Then came, in *Put-*

nam's Magazine, between 1852 and 1854, the satirical "Potiphar Papers" and the romantic "Prue and I"—the most imaginative and the loveliest of his books. After that the limitations of circumstance began to constrain him. He assumed the Easy Chair of *Harper's Magazine* in 1854,—receiving it from that Horatian classic of American letters Donald G. Mitchell, by whom it had just been started,—and he occupied it till the last. In *Harper's Weekly*, in 1859-60, he wrote the novel of "Trumps"—a work which will transmit to a distant future that typical American politician, prosperous and potential yesterday, to-day, and forever, General

Arcularius Belch. In *Harper's Bazar* he wrote a series of papers, extending over a period of four years, called " Manners on the Road "— the Road being life, and Manners being the conduct of people in their use of it. In those papers and in the Easy Chair the Addisonian drift of his mind was fully displayed. Those Essays do not excel *The Spectator* in thought, or learning, or humor, or invention, or in the thousand felicities of a courtly, leisurely, lace-ruffle style ; yet they are level with *The Spectator* in dignity of character and beauty of form ; they surpass it in vitality; and they surpass it in fertility of theme, sustained affluence of feeling, and diversity of literary grace. *The Spectator* contains 635 papers, and it was written by several hands, though mostly by the hand of Addison, between March 1710 and December 1714,—a period of four years and nine months. The Easy Chair contains over 2500 articles, and it was written by Curtis alone and was prolonged, with but one short intermission, for 38 years.

It was Wesley, the Methodist preacher, who objected to the custom of letting the devil have all the good music. Curtis was a moralist who objected to the custom of letting the rakes have all the graces. Good men are some times so insipid that they make virtue tedious. In Curtis, notwithstanding his invincible composure and perfect decorum, there was a strain of the gypsy. He had "heard the chimes at midnight" and he had not forgotten their music. He had been a wandering minstrel in his youth, and he had twanged the light guitar beneath the silver moon. As you turn the leaves of Lester Wallack's "Memories of Fifty Years," you find Curtis to be one of them ; you come upon him very pleasantly in the society of that brilliant actor, and you hear their youthful voices blended — the robust yet gentle genius of

Thackeray being a listener—in the golden cadence of Ben Jonson's lovely Grecian lyric :

" Drink to me only with thine eyes,
    And I will pledge with mine ;
Or leave a kiss but in the cup,
    And I'll not look for wine."

Throughout his life Curtis never lost the capacity for sentiment; the love of music ; the worship of art and beauty ; the morning glow of chivalrous emotion. He never became ascetic. He was a Puritan but he was not a bigot. He made the jest sparkle. He mingled in the dance. Without excess, but sweetly and genially, he filled a place at the festival. From his hand, in the remote days of the Castle Garden Opera, the glorious Jenny Lind received her first bouquet in America ; and from his lips, in the last year of his life, her illustrious memory received its sweetest tribute. When he heard the distant note of the street-organ his spirit floated away in a dream of " the mellow richness of Italy :" yet he was a man who could have ridden with Cromwell's troopers at Naseby, and given his life for freedom. There was no plainness of living to which he was not suited, and equally there was no opulence of culture and art that he could not wear with grace. The extremes of his character explain its power. There was no severity and no sacrifice of which he was not capable, in his scorn and detestation of evil and wrong; but for human frailty he had more than the tenderness of woman. He knelt with a disciple's reverence at the austere shrine of Washington : yet his eloquence blazed like morning sunlight upon a wilderness of roses when he touched the rugged, mournful, humorous, pathetic story of Robert Burns.

In this evanescent and vanishing world one thing, and only one thing, endures,—the spiritual influence of good. Out of nature, out of literature, out of art, out of character, that alone, transmuted into conduct, survives ensphered when all the rest has perished. We are accustomed, unconsciously, to speak of our possessions and our deprivations as if we ourselves were permanent ; not remembering that, in a very little while, our places also will be empty. Our friend is dead—our champion, our benefactor, our guide ! Life will be lonelier without his presence. The streets in which he used to walk seem vacant. The very air of our silent and slumberous island, musing at the mysterious gateways of the sea, seems more brooding and more solitary. Yet, being dead, he far more truly lives than we do, and in far more exceeding glory, because in that potential influence which can never die. Still in our rambles he will meet us, with the old familiar look that always seemed to say, 'You also are a prince, an emperor, a man; you also possess this wonderful heritage of beauty, and honor, and immortal life.' Still in the homes of the poor will dwell the memory of his inexhaustible goodness. Still in the abodes of the rich will live the sweetness and the power of his benignant

example : and still, when we
have passed away and have been
forgotten, a distant posterity,
remembering the illustrious orator, the wise and gentle philosopher, the serene and delicate
literary artist, the incorruptible
patriot, the supreme gentleman,
will cherish the writings, will
revere the character, and will
exult in the splendid tradition of
George William Curtis.

I shall close this address with
the Monody that I wrote not long
after his death:

I.

ALL the flowers were in their pride
On the day when Rupert died.

Dreamily, through dozing trees
Sighed the idle summer breeze.

Wild birds, glancing through the air,
Spilled their music everywhere.

Not one sign of mortal ill
Told that his great heart was still.

Now the grass he loved to tread
Murmurs softly o'er his head:

Now the great green branches wave
High above his lonely grave:

While in grief's perpetual speech
Roll the breakers on the beach.

O my comrade, O my friend,
Must this parting be the end?

II.

Weave the shroud and spread the
  pall!
Night and silence cover all.

Howsoever we deplore,
They who go return no more.

Never from that unknown track
Floats one answering whisper back.

Nature, vacant, will not heed
Lips that grieve or hearts that bleed.

Wherefore now should mourning word
Or the tearful dirge be heard?

How shall words our grief abate?—
Call him noble; call him great;

Say that faith, now gaunt and grim,
Once was fair because of him;

Say that goodness, round his way,
Made one everlasting day;

Say that beauty's heavenly flame
Bourgeoned wheresoe'er he came;

Say that all life's common ways
Were made glorious in his gaze;

Say he gave us, hour by hour,
Hope and patience, grace and power;

Say his spirit was so true
That it made us noble too;—

What is this, but to declare
Life's bereavement, Love's despair?

What is this, but just to say
All we loved is torn away?

Weave the shroud and spread the
    pall!
Night and silence cover all.

III.

O my comrade, O my friend,
Must this parting be the end?

Heart and hope are growing old:
Dark the night comes down, and
    cold:

Few the souls that answer mine,
And no voice so sweet as thine.

Desert wastes of care remain—
Yet thy lips speak not again!

Gray eternities of space—
Yet nowhere thy living face!

Only now the lonesome blight,
Heavy day and haunted night.

All the light and music reft—
Only thought and memory left!

Peace, fond mourner! This thy
      boon,—
Thou thyself must follow soon.

Peace,—and let repining go!
Peace,—for Fate will have it so.

Vainly now his praise is said;
Vain the garland for his head:

Yet is comfort's shadow cast
From the kindness of the past.

All my love could do to cheer
Warmed his heart when he was here.

Honor's plaudit, friendship's vow
Did not coldly wait till now.

O my comrade, O my friend,
If this parting be the end,

Yet I hold my life divine
To have known a soul like thine:

And I hush the low lament,
In submission, penitent.

Still the sun is in the skies:
He sets—but I have seen him rise!

APPENDIX.

The following tribute to the memory of Curtis was written by me, in the New York *Tribune* of September 1, 1892,—the morning after his death. —W. W.

" AMONG American men of letters no man of this generation has so completely filled as Curtis did the ideal of clear intellect, pure taste, moral purpose, chivalry of feeling, and personal refinement and grace. From the moment of his entrance into public life, as a speaker,—now nearly forty years ago,—he has entirely satisfied, especially for the mind of sensitive and generous youth, the highest conception of purity, dignity, and sweetness. His noble presence and serious demeanor, the repose and sweep and sway of his eloquence, and the crystal clearness of his literary style were all felt to be naturally and spontaneously representative of an exalted personality. Upon all public occasions the tremulous sensibility of his feelings and the inflexible reticence of his mind were not less remarkable than the absolute propriety and perfect symmetry of his language. In the element of felicity few orators have equalled him and no orator has surpassed him. He was, of course, an artist; but the soul of his art was the virtuous and wise sincerity of a noble nature. The work was fine, but the man was finer than the work; and of all the charms that he exerted none was so great as that of his pure and gentle spirit. His manners, indeed, were so undemonstrative and so polished as to seem cold; but all who knew him, all who ever listened to his speech, felt and owned in him the spell of inherent, genuine nobility.

There is, indeed, a conception of character and conduct which assumes that when a man is not effusive and familiar he is aristocratic. Curtis was reticent: yet no one ever more profoundly and practically believed than he did in the brotherhood of humanity. He was republican, through and through. His voice and his pen, his personal influence and his private means, were always enlisted in the cause of the helpless, the oppressed, and the weak. Perhaps the best oration he ever delivered was that upon Robert Burns—in which every word thrills with the pulsation of human kindness, and of which the spirit is love for every virtue and pity for every weakness of the human race. But his theory of equality was not degradation. He desired, and he labored, to equalize the race, not by dragging people down, but by raising them up. If he was fastidious and reticent, he did not deny to others the right to be fastidious and reticent also. In this he was of the kindred of Bryant, and Washington Irving, and Longfellow, and Emerson,— with whom he had much in common, and the spotless standard of whose art and life he loyally and brilliantly sustained and has transmitted in light and beauty to all the younger men of letters who succeed him. In all that the word implies he was a gentleman; and there is no worthier or more expressive tribute that can be brought to any man's coffin than the tear that will not be repressed for life-long devotion to duty, for goodness that never faltered and kindness that never failed.

In the presence of death and under the instant sense of bereavement it is not easily possible to speak with cold judgment of his achievements as a writer. He was the master of a style as pure as that of Addison and as flexible as that of Lamb. In its characteristic quality, however, it does not resemble either of those models. The influences that were most intimately concerned in forming his mind were Emerson and Thackeray. He had the broad vision and the fresh, brave, aspiring spirit of the one, and he combined with those the satirical playfulness, the cordial detestation of shams, and the subtle commingling of raillery and tender sentiment that are characteristic of the other. His habitual mood was pensive, not passionate, and he was essentially more a contemplative philosopher than either an advocate, a partisan, a reformer, or a politician—all of which parts he sometimes was constrained to assume. He was born for the vocation of letters and his best success was gained in the literary art. His literature will survive in the affectionate admiration of his countrymen long after his political papers are forgotten. 'Prue and I' is one of the most delicate, dreamlike books in our language, and the spirit that it discloses is full of romance, tenderness and beauty. The affectionate heart, the lively fancy, and the subtle literary instinct of Goldsmith could not have made it finer. As an orator he had all the grace and more than the emotion of Everett, whose tradition he has perpetuated. His rhetoric was not merely a sheen of words, but it burned and shimmered with the vital splendor of a sincere heart. He was in earnest in all that he said and did. He has had a long and good life, and his name is noble forever.

www.ingramcontent.com/pod-product-compliance
Lightning Source LLC
Chambersburg PA
CBHW020802020726
47495CB00008B/2554

*9 7 8 3 7 4 3 4 4 4 0 1 0 *